The Big Freeze

Based on the stories by Marvel Comics
By Billy Wrecks
Illustrated by Michael Borkowski and Michael Atiyeh

© 2013 MARVEL
marvelkids.com

 A GOLDEN BOOK • NEW YORK

All rights reserved. Published in the United States by Golden Books, an imprint of Random House Children's Books, a division of Penguin Random House LLC, 1745 Broadway, New York, NY 10019, and in Canada by Penguin Random House Canada Limited, Toronto. Golden Books, A Golden Book, A Little Golden Book, the G colophon, and the distinctive gold spine are registered trademarks of Penguin Random House LLC.
rhcbooks.com
ISBN 978-0-307-97656-7 (trade) — ISBN 978-0-399-55928-0 (ebook)
Printed in the United States of America
15 14 13 12 11 10

The Amazing **Spider-Man** was swinging through New York City when his spider-sense started tingling.

"There's trouble in the park—and as usual, it's headed *my* way," Spider-Man said. "I wonder who it will be today—the Green Goblin? Aliens? Doctor Doom?"

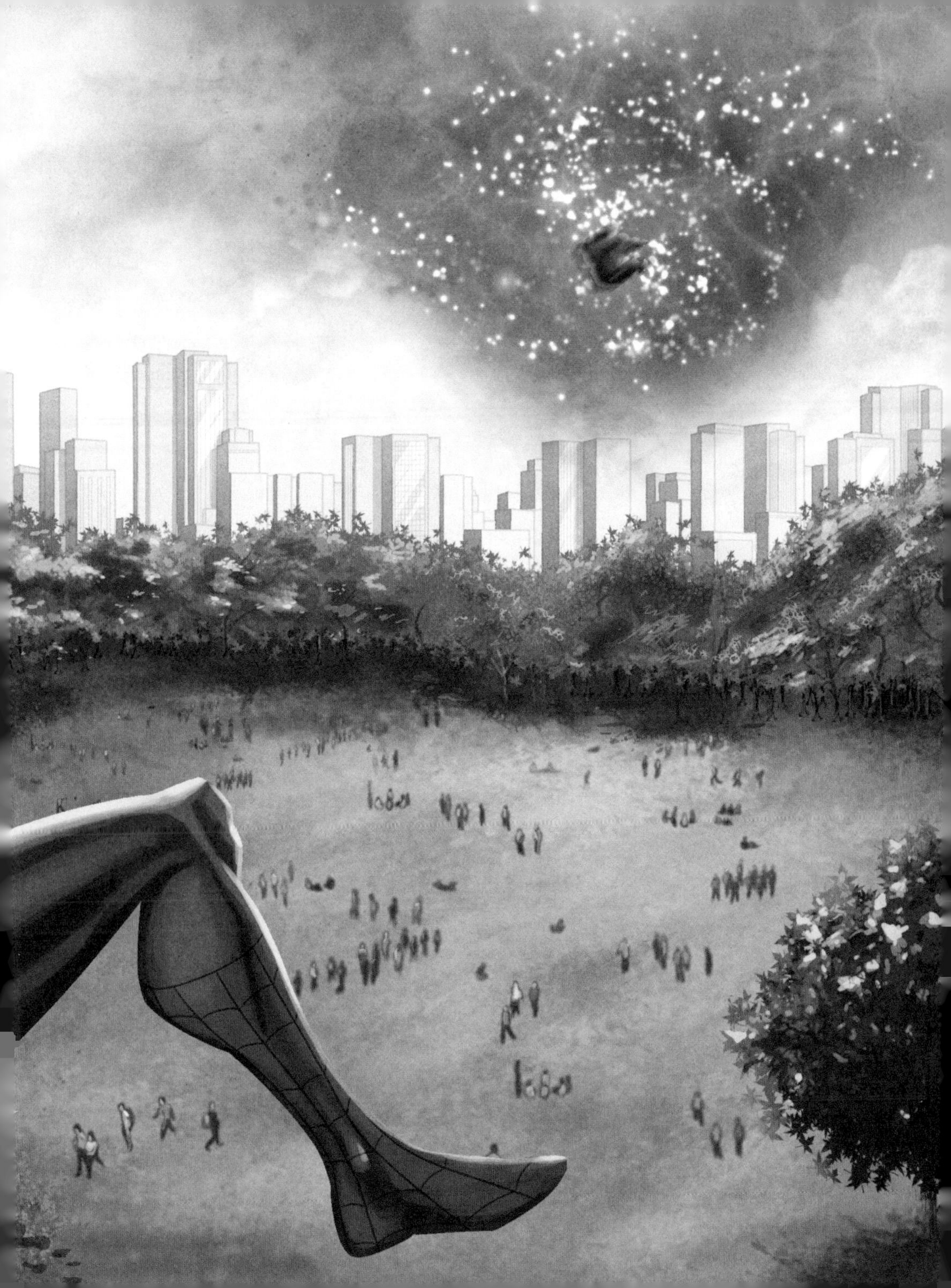

GRRR!

Spider-Man jumped out of the way as a huge green blur hurtled past him.
Now I know there's trouble! Spider-Man thought.

The big green blur smashed into the street. It was the Incredible **Hulk**.

"Now Hulk is angry," the green giant growled. "Make Hulk want to **SMASH!**"

"Whoa, big fella. What happened?" Spider-Man asked. "Big blue men came through hole in the sky," Hulk snarled. "Blue men look for Hulk's friend, blond hair."

"Blue men? Blond hair? What are you talking about?"
Spider-Man replied as enormous shadows loomed over
them. "And why is it getting dark? Uh-oh."

Spider-Man looked up. Three fierce **Frost Giants**
from the distant realm of Asgard towered above them.
"We are looking for Thor," boomed the leader of
the Frost Giants—who was also the biggest. "And I will
cover this city with ice and snow until he faces us!"

Suddenly, a repulsor ray blasted one of the Frost Giants. It was—

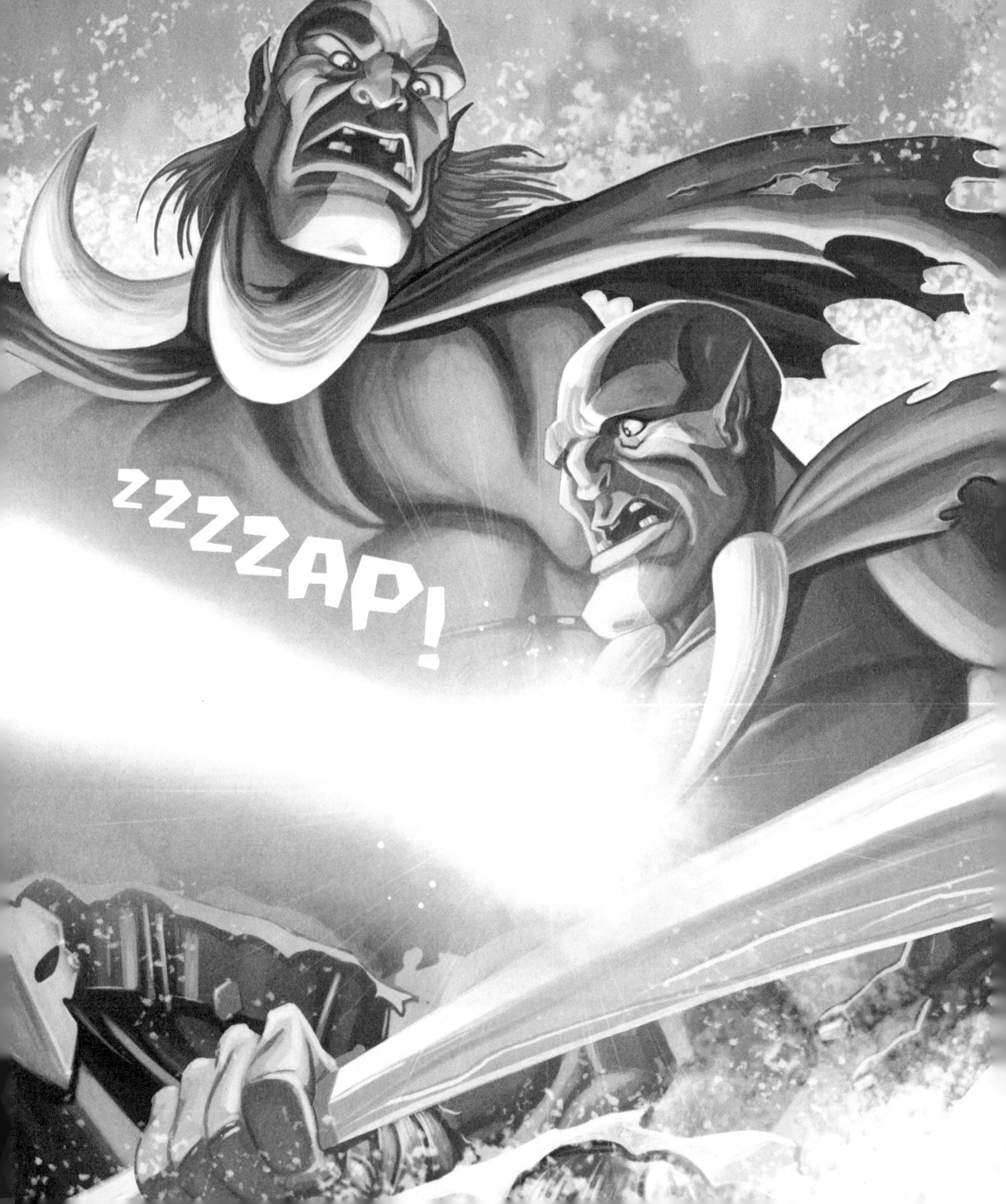
ZZZZAP!

Iron Man!

"Thor is on the way," Iron Man warned the Frost Giants. "But until he gets here, you will just have to deal with . . .

. . . us!”

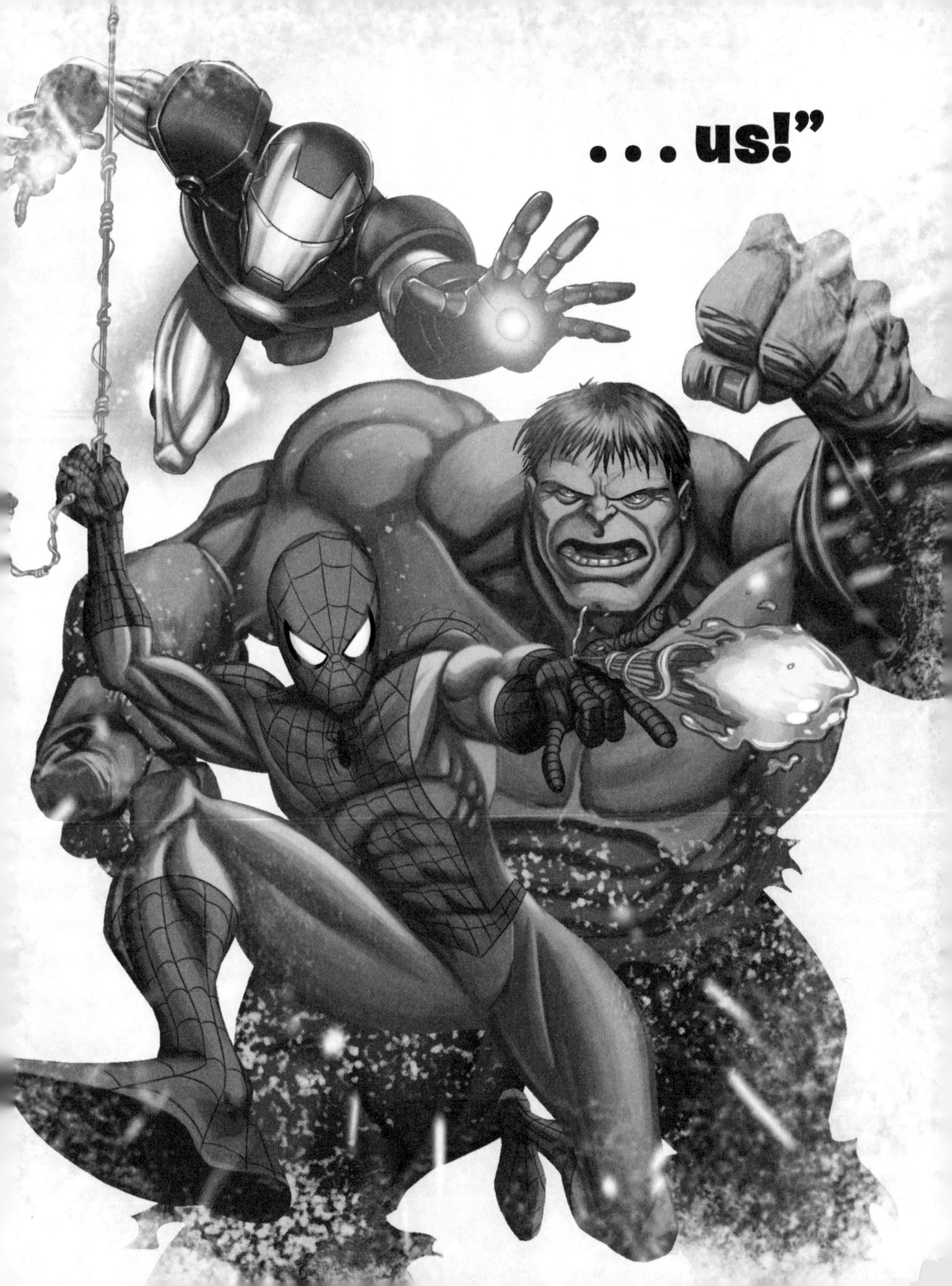

As the biggest Frost Giant continued to summon more snow, Iron Man, Spider-Man, and Hulk bravely fought the foes. But the Frost Giants were very big and very strong!

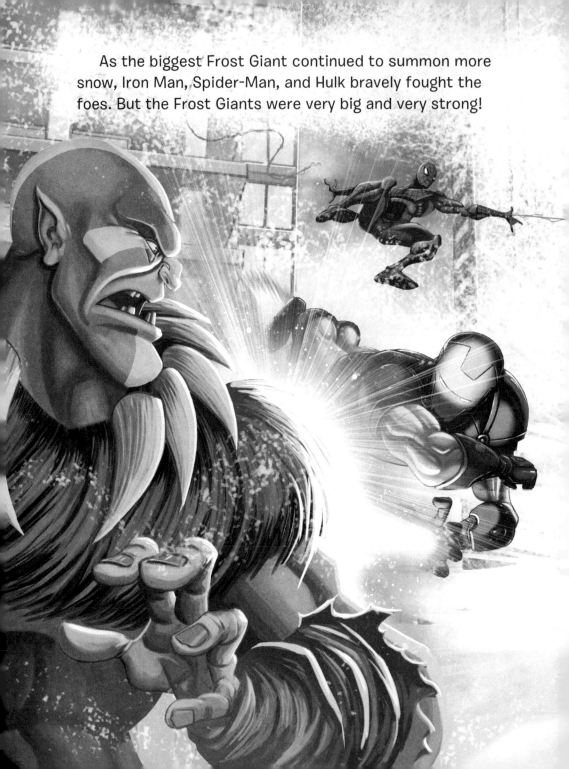

"I thought the bigger they were, the harder they fell!"
Spider-Man joked.

"Less talk. More SMASH, Bug Man!" Hulk growled.

"Brrr," Spider-Man said, covering the biggest Frost Giant with his web. "You better wrap up before you catch a cold."

"Let's lead the Frost Giants back to the park, where they won't cause as much damage," Iron Man suggested.

"Good idea, Shell Head," Spider-Man replied. "Hulk said something about a hole in the sky. Maybe it's the portal they came through."

Suddenly, thunder rumbled and lightning flashed!

"Laufey!" **Thor** roared at the biggest Frost Giant. "What is the meaning of this?"

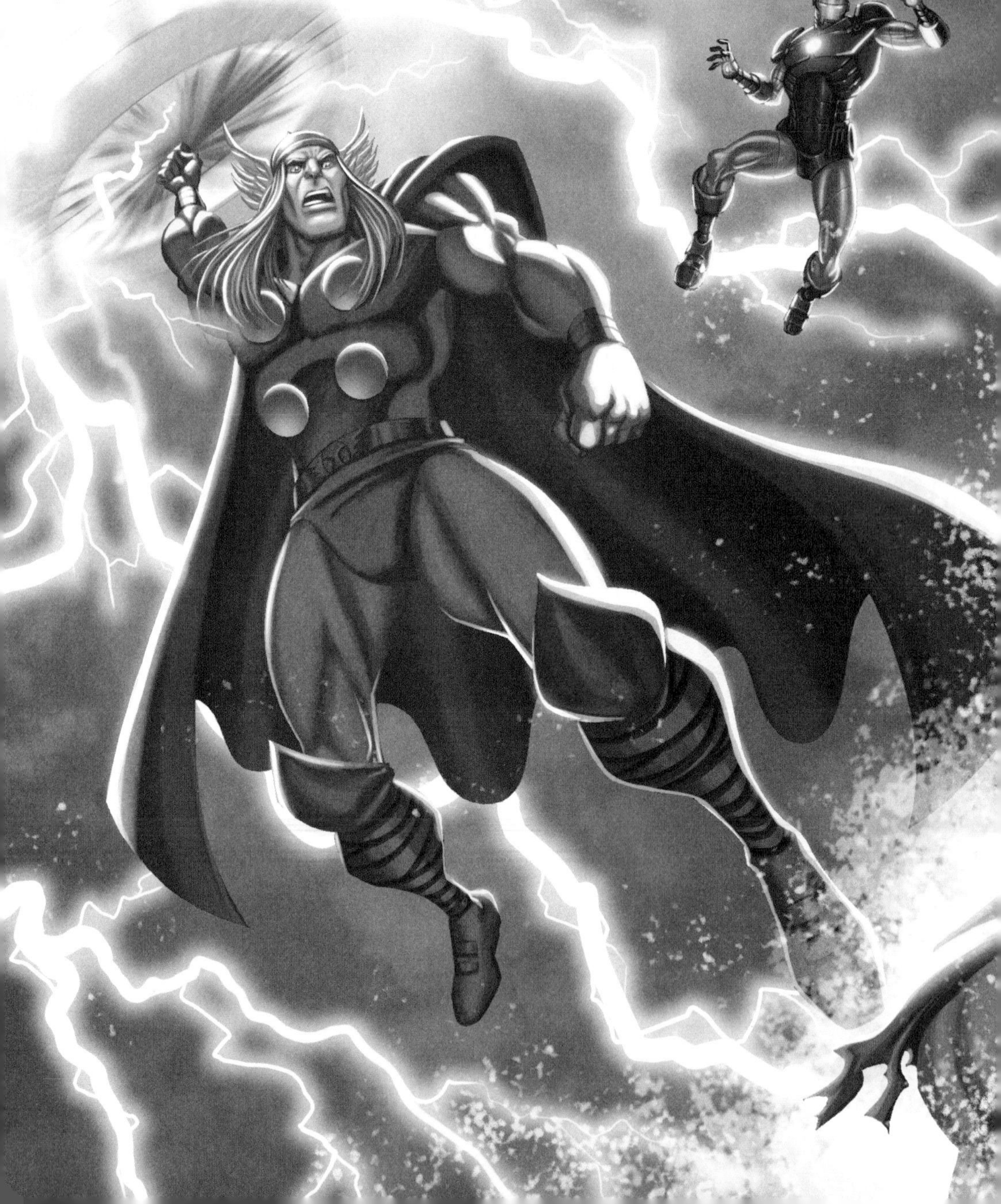

“The last time we met, on that snowy battlefield, you were victorious,” Laufey snarled. “I promised to get even. And today I shall!”

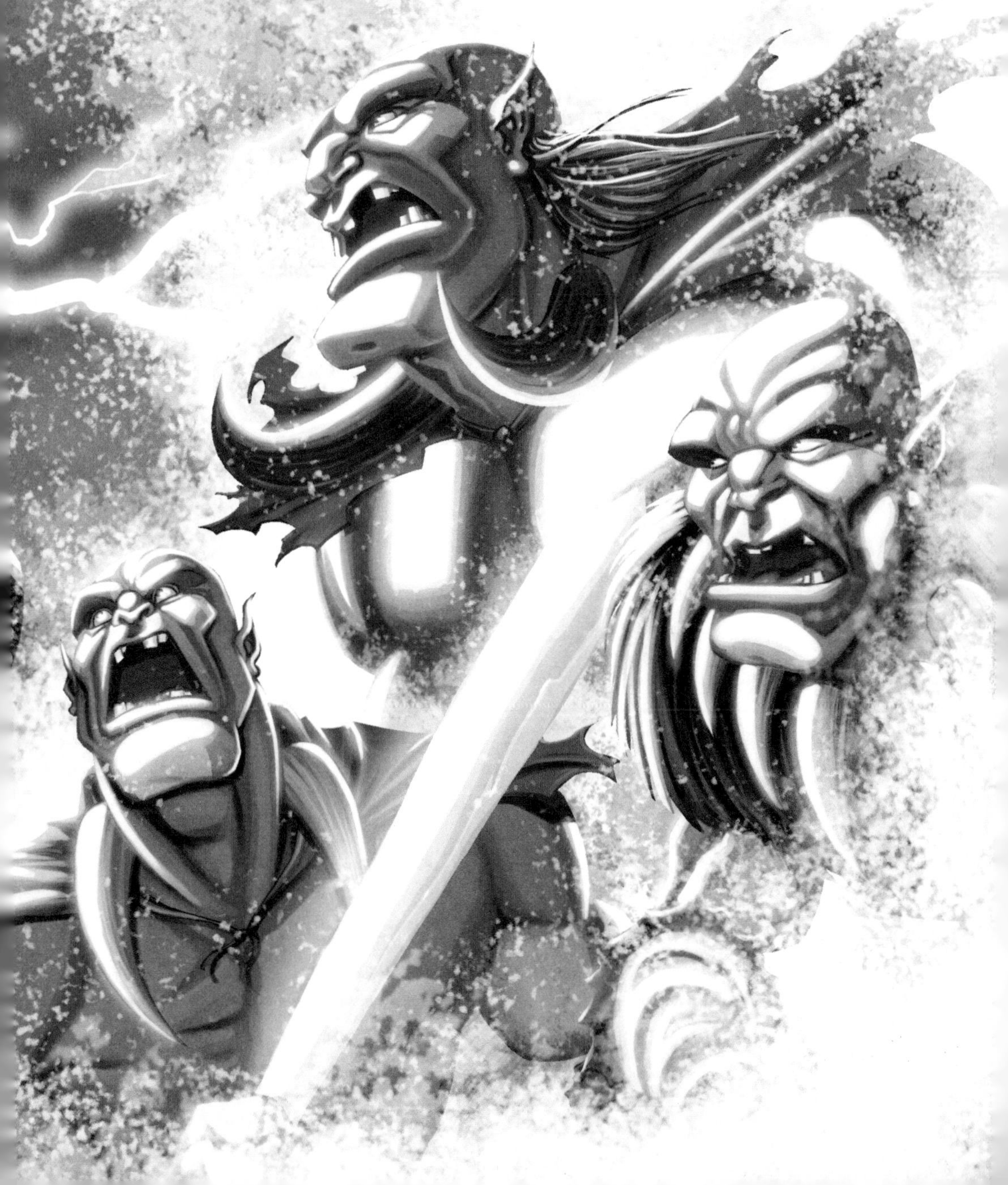

Without warning, Laufey hurled a big, frosty snowball at Thor with blinding speed!

Thor swung his mighty hammer and smashed the snowball.
Ice splattered everywhere!

SPLAT!

"Gotcha!" Laufey roared gleefully. Then all three
Frost Giants dashed for the open portal in the sky.

"HA! HA!" Thor laughed heartily. "Well struck,
Frost Giants! But this time I have my friends. Join me, heroes!"

The heroes quickly jumped into the snowball fight
with the Frost Giants. Even the people of New York helped!
Thor chased the Frost Giants back to their portal.
As it closed behind them, everyone cheered!

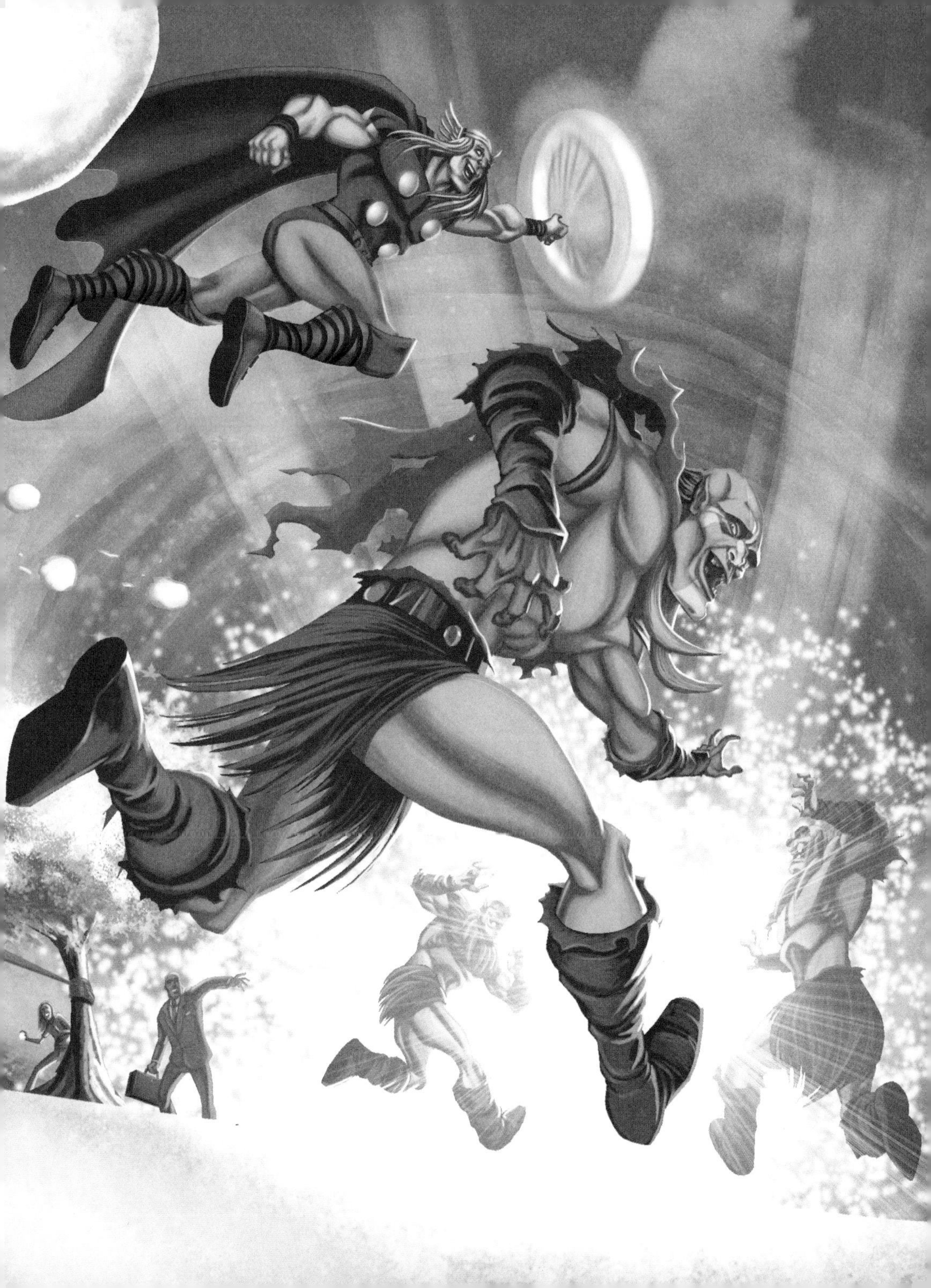

"The Frost Giants are gone, but the city is still covered in snow," Spider-Man said to Hulk and Iron Man. "I guess there's only one thing to do—**DUCK!**"